I Have a Sister

by Smiljana Čoh

tiger tales

This is my sister.

She is very small.

A long time ago,
I was small too.

Now I am BIG.

My sister is happy
to have me because
I make her smile.

I teach her
things I know.

I can swing,

dance,

skate, and

stack blocks.

I help Mommy bathe her.

When I was little,
Mommy bathed me too.

Now I can splash
in the big bathtub.

My sister
loves to
be carried.

When I
was small,
I loved to be
carried too.

Now I can carry my dolls and stuffed animals. I give them rides in my wagon.

My sister can't talk yet.
But she can listen.

I tell her stories.

When she gets bigger, we will do all of my favorite things together . . .

because she's my sister
and I love her sooo much!